The Empress of Salt and Fortune

THE EMPRESS OF SALT AND FORTUNE

NGHI VO

A TOM DOHERTY ASSOCIATES BOOK

NEW YORK

THE EMPRESS OF SALT AND FORTUNE

Copyright © 2020 by Nghi Vo

Cover art by Alyssa Winans
Cover design by Christine Foltzer

Edited by Ruoxi Chen

A Tor.com Book
Published by Tom Doherty Associates
120 Broadway
New York, NY 10271

www.tor.com

Tor® is a registered trademark of
Macmillan Publishing Group, LLC.

ISBN 978-1-250-75029-7 (ebook)
ISBN 978-1-250-75030-3 (trade paperback)

First Edition: March 2020

For my family

The Empress of Salt and Fortune

Chapter One

"Something wants to eat you," called Almost Brilliant from her perch in a nearby tree, "and I shall not be sorry if it does."

Chiming bells. Chih rolled to their feet, glancing around the perimeter and squinting at the jangling string of bells that surrounded the small campsite. For a moment, they were back at the abbey in Singing Hills, late for another round of prayers, chores, and lessons, but Singing Hills did not smell of ghosts and damp pine boughs. Singing Hills did not make the hairs on Chih's arms rise up in alarm or their heart lurch with panic.

The bells were still again.

"Whatever it is, it's passed. It's safe to come down."

The hoopoe chirped something that managed to convey both suspicion and exasperation in a two-tone call, but she came down to settle on Chih's head, shifting uneasily.

"The protections must still be up. We are very close to Lake Scarlet now."

"We wouldn't even have gotten this far if they were."

Chih considered for a moment, and then they stepped into their sandals and ducked under the belled string.

Almost Brilliant fluttered up in alarm before coming down to land on Chih's shoulder this time.

"Cleric Chih, get back to your campsite! You are going to get killed, and then I will have to tell the Divine how terribly irresponsible you were."

"Be sure to make a good account of it," Chih said absently. "Hush now; I think I can see what made that racket."

The hoopoe made a disgruntled rustling noise, but she dug her claws more firmly into Chih's shoulder. Despite their bravado, the neixin's feathery weight on their shoulder was a comfort, and Chih reached up to stroke her crest gently before walking between the pines.

They knew that there was no road there. They had crossed the white pine copse earlier that day, and though they could see the remnants of a road underneath the overgrown bracken and fallen boughs, it wouldn't have let a dogcart through. Chih suspected that the road had once connected Lake Scarlet to the royal highway, in the days before the lake had been taken off every map and effectively disappeared by a highly dedicated and skilled imperial sorcerer.

There was no road there during the day, but obviously at night, things were different. The road ran as broad as a barge through the trees, and ranged on either side were faded ghosts, the former guardians of Lake Scarlet. Even a few months ago, Chih knew, the ghosts would have fallen on any living thing that crossed their path, tearing them to pieces and then crying because they were still so hungry.

Now, though, they had eyes for nothing but the palanquin coming down the ghost road from the east, the direction of Lake Scarlet. It was borne by six veiled men. Their feet did not quite touch the ground. In the moonlight, it was all silvered, but Chih could tell that by all rights, it should be swathed in imperial red and gold, the mammoth and lion of the empire embroidered in lavish detail on the curtains.

There was only one woman in the world who had the right to show the mammoth and the lion, and she was to be crowned in her first Dragon Court in the capital.

Well, thought Chih, curling their hand around Almost Brilliant for comfort, only one living woman.

Chih bowed as low as the ghosts around them as the palanquin went by, wishing with all their might that the late empress would open the drapes and show her face. Would it be the wrinkled woman swathed in thick silks Chih had once glimpsed as a child on Houksen, or would it be a far younger woman, the Empress of Salt and Fortune as she had first come to Anh, before the end of the eternal summer and before the mammoth had trampled the lion?

When Chih straightened, ghosts and road and empress were gone, leaving nothing behind but Chih's own pounding heart.

"Did you see that?" they asked Almost Brilliant, who had finally stopped shivering.

"Yes," said the hoopoe, her normally shrill tone subdued. "That was worth being terrified that you were going to die in a truly terrible fashion."

Chih laughed, smoothing a finger over Almost Brilliant's crest, and starting the short walk back to their campsite.

"Come on. We can get a few more hours of sleep before we need to pack up and start walking again."

It took another two days' walk through the birch barrens before they came to the narrow beach of Lake Scarlet at dusk. The lake itself was almost perfectly circular, formed from the death of a falling star, and farther down the beach Chih saw the low green-tiled roof of the former empress's compound. To their surprise, there was a lantern lit on the porch built over the water.

"Don't tell me it's looters already?"

As they watched, however, an old woman came walking out of the house with a smart step, and when she reached the railing, she stared out over the water and at the indigo sky above, where the stars were stepping forward. Chih was just wondering what to do when the old woman caught sight of them.

"Come over! You can see the lake better from here!"

Almost Brilliant kept her own counsel, so Chih picked their way along the rocky shore of the beach, coming up the shallow steps to the porch just as the last salmon light was leaving the sky. The old woman gestured for them to come closer.

"Come, you're just in time."

She indicated that Chih was meant to help themself from the small dish of sesame crackers on the railing, but she herself looked distracted, gazing over the black water and holding one cracker in her hand. After a few moments, she turned down the lantern wick until it emitted only a sullen glow.

"Grandmother, I'm here to—"

"Shush, girl, it's happening."

Above was the rapidly darkening sky. All around them was the darkness of the birch barrens, and spread out before them was Lake Scarlet, like a mirror reflecting nothing but night. At first, Chih thought it was their imagination, nothing more than a mirage that came after staring at something too hard, but then they realized that it was real. There was a faint glow coming from the water itself, something like the very last gleam of a dying hearth fire.

"What—"

"Shh. Watch. Just watch."

Chih held their breath as the soft red glow brightened, sweeping across the lake like the sparks of New Year fireworks. It was brilliant, too hard to look at so very closely, and it flooded the water, enough so they could make out individual trees on the beach, the black silhouette of the night birds on the water, and the seamed face of the woman standing next to them, creased in pleasure.

"I was hoping it would go tonight. It's still a little cold yet, but it has come even earlier in some years."

Chih stood side by side with the woman, staring out over the pyrotechnic display before them. Just a short while after the red lights came up to their full brightness, they started to dim again. Chih counted in their head. When they had reached one hundred, there was only a faint reddish glow to the water.

The old woman sighed happily as she turned the lamp back up.

"Every time, it is like the first, and I have not seen it in sixty years. Come inside; it's still too cold for my brittle bones."

Chih was old enough to know that no one was harmless, and still young enough to obey instantly that tone of command from an older woman. They followed her into the residence, where she lit several paper lamps. There was a damp chill to the small room they sat in, but the light helped a little. They sat together on the leather cushions around the empty hearth, and the old woman looked a little closer at Chih, taking in their shaved head, belled string, and indigo robes.

"Oh, I see I was mistaken. Not a girl at all, but a cleric." Chih smiled.

"It's an easy mistake, grandmother, but yes. I am Cleric Chih from the Singing Hills abbey. This little feathery menace is Almost Brilliant."

Almost Brilliant whooped in indignation at being so described and showed off her manners by alighting in front of their hostess and tocking the boards in front of her twice with her narrow beak.

"Most honored to make your acquaintance, matriarch," Almost Brilliant said in her grumbling gravelly voice.

"And I yours, Mistress Almost Brilliant. If your cleric is from the Singing Hills, you must be a neixin, are you not?"

Almost Brilliant's feathers fluffed out in pride. "Yes, matriarch. I am descended from the line of Ever Victorious and Always Kind. Our memories go all the way back to the Xun Dynasty."

"What a pleasure. They killed so many of your kind during the reign of Emperor Sung. I was not sure I would ever see another."

"The Singing Hills aviary was torched, but our Divine at the time sent three pairs of nesting couples to their relatives across the Hu River," said Chih. "Among them were Almost Brilliant's great-grandparents. If you know about neixin, grandmother, you must know how they need to have a place and a name for everything."

"And I imagine you do as well, don't you, cleric? Very well. My family name is Sun, but I have always been called Rabbit." She grinned, showing two teeth that were indeed longer than the ones around them.

"Children used to tease me about it when I was young, but I am very old now, and I have never lost a single tooth."

Almost Brilliant whistled in satisfaction, and Chih grinned.

"Welcome to your place in history, grandmother. Do you live nearby? I didn't think anyone was likely to beat me to Lake Scarlet when the word came down about the declassification."

"I have family that run an inn along the road. It's funny. The locals think the area is cursed from the red glow of the lake, but I've always thought it beautiful. Like bonfires and fireworks. But now that you are here, and Almost Brilliant as well, I am pleased that the true history of Lake Scarlet will be told."

Chih smiled at Rabbit's words. She sounded a little like the former Divine, who had always encouraged their acolytes to speak to the florists and the bakers as much as to the warlords and magistrates. *Accuracy above all things. You will never remember the great if you do not remember the small.*

"I am due in the capital for the eclipse next month and the new empress's first Dragon Court, but I was at Kailin when the word came down that all of the sites put under imperial lock during Empress In-yo's reign were being declassified. I was so close to Lake Scarlet that I couldn't resist."

Rabbit laughed in a friendly way.

"Couldn't resist being the first to unearth Thriving Fortune's secrets, either, could you, Cleric Chih?"

"I won't deny that ambition has its part to play in my stopping, but I have never heard the name Thriving Fortune before, grandmother."

"You wouldn't. It is what the female attendants of Empress In-yo called it when they first came here from the capital. It was a joke, you see. They were all of the court, and it was a bitter thing indeed for them to be sent into the wilderness with a barbarian empress."

Chih sat very still, and next to them, Almost Brilliant cocked her head to one side.

"It sounds like you knew of them, grandmother."

Rabbit snorted.

"Of course I did. I came all this way with them, and it was I who told them to hire my father to come up every week with supplies from the main road. They never knew to tip him, or perhaps they thought their cosmopolitan beauty was tip enough. Pah!"

"I would be grateful, grandmother, for any stories you could tell me of the empress's time here at Lake Scarlet. I do not have any money, but I will be more than happy to share my food with you, and if you have any chores that need to be done—."

"No, cleric, save your food and your labor. This house is very old, and you will have your work cut out for you if you want to be in the capital for the eclipse. But now I am tired, and I should retire."

She blew out all save two lanterns, picking one up to carry comfortably in her hand.

"You may take the other and choose whatever room you care to take. I always get up early, and I will be happy to help you with whatever your work entails."

She padded into the darker reaches of the house, and Chih and Almost Brilliant listened as her shushing footsteps faded into nothing.

"I would go outside if only there were not owls in the pines," Almost Brilliant said unhappily. "I do not like the roof over this place."

"And I'm not sure I care for the rest, but at least we have been made welcome."

After a little bit of exploring, they found a storage room nearby, small enough that Chih could stretch out flat on the floor and feel the walls around all sides. They spread their bedroll on the polished wooden floor, and then carefully and deliberately, they hung their string of bells across the closed panel of the door.

Above them in the rafters, Almost Brilliant made a roost close to the eaves, watching but saying nothing. When Chih finally drifted off, a fold of their robe tucked around their body against the spring chill, they did not dream of ghouls or ghosts, but instead of sunlight on bright water and a rabbit nosing at the makeup stand of a fine lady.

Chapter Two

Robe. Silk, silk thread, ruby bead. Green background em-
broidered with darker green leaves. A single red ruby
beetle bead rests on a green leaf on the right arm.
Sleeping robe. Silk, muslin, and silk thread. Mulberry
muslin edged with white silk, the archaic characters
for "Restful Sleep" embroidered inside the collar.
Tunic. White fur, black fur, suede, and ivory. White fur
striped with black along the sleeves. A pattern of
waves has been shaved into the fur. The inside is lined
with suede, and the throat closed with an ivory toggle.

"That's a tooth."

Chih and Almost Brilliant looked up as Rabbit came in with four small bowls on a tray. One was filled with fatty scraps that she set in front of Almost Brilliant, who flapped down from the rafters to peck at them with pleasure.

"A tooth?" asked Chih, touching the ivory carefully. It was smooth under their fingers and carved with curling lines that hurt their eyes when they looked at it too closely.

The entire sealskin tunic was made with consummate skill, but it was easily as heavy on its own as any four of the silk dresses that were bundled in the cedar chest with it.

"Yes. Come eat some pounded rice, and I shall tell you what the empress told me."

Chih came to sit across from Rabbit with the tray between them. They had not lost their wariness from the night before, but in daylight, Rabbit looked like so many of the lay sisters who were constantly in and out of the abbey, as much fixtures as the stone hoopoes that studded the walls or the smell of wood pulp being milled into sheets of paper.

The pounded rice was still warm and flavored with birch water, and the two of them ate companionably for a while, scooping the rice into their mouths with spooned fingers and cleaning them in the bowl of water. Rabbit rinsed her bowl neatly before setting it aside, and she smiled at the white seal-fur dress as if it were an old acquaintance spotted in the marketplace.

~

I suppose you have guessed by now that I am quite at home in this old place. It is true that my family is from this region, but when I was only five, the county sent me along with one hundred san of birch water, thirty young goats, and fifty caskets of orange dye to the capital. It was meant to be fifty-five caskets of dye, you see, and they hoped if they sent me along that the tax collectors would be forgiving.

I suppose they were, and I spent the next four years scrubbing the Palace of Gleaming Light, never raising my head. I got to know the palace by the baseboards, the wood of the floors, the smell of the paper screens, and the way that lamp oil burned all night, never letting the darkness approach His Most Divine Presence the Emperor of Pine and Steel, Emperor Sung.

I might have been a rabbit-toothed girl from the provinces, but I worked so well that when I was ten, I had been promoted to cleaning the women's quarters. I was so proud when they gave me the veil that marked me as one of the servants of the inner house. If I could have written then, I would have written to my father and mother of how their daughter, veiled and wearing household green, was lined up along the Paulwonia Hall with two hundred others to greet the new empress from the north.

The royal household agency positioned us before dawn, prowling up and down the lines as nervously as cats and lashing out with their horsehair whips when we slouched or yawned. More than one girl fainted, but I was a strong thing, and I stood like a statue until past noon, when there was a great commotion in the courtyard. We knew from the snapping of banners and the shouts of the guards that the empress had arrived.

She did not come, as her late mother had once threatened, with a battalion of mammoths to bring down the walls of the Palace of Gleaming Light. Instead, she had come with only an honor guard that was barred from the inner palace, and so she walked down the long hallway to the court of the emperor all alone.

We had been scolded and smacked and told that if we raised our eyes to the future mother of the emperor we would be relegated to cleaning the kitchen refuse pits. I could not help myself, however, and I glanced up to see her pass by.

History will say that she was an ugly woman, but that is not true. She had a foreigner's beauty, like a language we do not know how to read. She was barely taller than I was at ten, and built like an ox drover's daughter. Her two long braids hung over her shoulders as black as ink, and her face was as flat as a dish and almost perfectly round. Pearl-faced, they call it where she came from, but piggish is what they called it here.

She walked past with her spine like one of these birch trees, and she wore this dress, which is as white today as it was then.

The seal that the dress was made from was killed by her brother on his first hunt. Patient as the unending ice itself, he had stalked it for days at the breathing holes where they come up, and when it rose, it was as large as a man. The toggle is one of its teeth, carved by her uncle. Her brother and uncle, whose names are now only spoken in the mortuary halls of Ingrusk, were killed just a year before, at the battle of Ko-anam Fords.

She would bring with her a wealth of salt, bushels of pearls, and enough whale oil to keep the palace alight for twenty years or more, one of the finest dowries ever to come to an emperor of Anh, but that was still a week away. When she first came to the Palace of Gleaming Light, In-yo was alone and empty-handed, wearing a splendid seal-fur dress that the ladies of the women's quarters could only call strange and barbaric.

She never wore this dress again in the palace, but when the emperor sent her into exile, she asked me to pack it carefully. I was thirteen then, and it was my job to look after it. I packaged it so carefully between layers and layers of crisp paper, and every ten days I brought it out to brush away any possible moth eggs or larvae.

Even though there was a fashion for seal fur in the capital when In-yo became the empress in truth, there never was a dress like this one again. There could never be. It is beautiful, but every stitch bites into her history, the deaths she left behind her, and the home she could not return to.

Do you understand?

~

"I am not sure I do, grandmother, but I listen, and Almost Brilliant will remember."

Rabbit flinched a little, as if she had forgotten herself. For a single faraway moment, she looked like something other than a simple servant woman, but it was there and gone so fast that Chih could not say for sure what it was.

"That is your calling, isn't it? To remember and to mark down."

"It is. Sometimes the things we see do not make sense until many years have gone by. Sometimes it takes generations. We are taught to be content with that."

Rabbit tilted her head, looking at Chih carefully.

"Are you? Content with that, I mean?"

"After my novitiate, they sent me to the kingdom of Sen, where Almost Brilliant and I were to take an account of their summer water festival. We were just meant to be there to record populations, dances, fireworks, things like that, but on the ninth day of the festival, a brown carp cleared the final gate of the city's dams and became a calico dragon. It twisted over the city, bringing down a month of holy rain, and then it was gone. Grandmother, I am very content."

Rabbit smiled, standing to pick up the dishes and to offer Almost Brilliant a gentle stroke along her crest.

"Good."

That night Chih dreamed of a man in a field of blinding white, waiting at a breathing hole with the patience of the damned for a seal to come up. In their dream, the man heard a call and then, with a smile on his round face, he turned and walked away, leaving his spear behind.

Chapter Three

Cup. Polished mahogany inlaid with silver. A silver spider
is inlaid into the bottom of the cup.
Five cubed dice. Bone and gold. The figures inscribed in
silver on each side include the moon, a woman, a fish,
a cat, a ship, and a needle.
Game board. Pale wood and gold paint. Drawn in six cir-
cles are the moon, a woman, a fish, a cat, a ship, and a
needle.

Chih smiled faintly at the game they'd pulled from underneath a sleeping platform, tucked among dusty extra
bedding and a half-dozen pairs of extra slippers, all alike.
They tumbled the dice into the cup, rattling them to
make a hollow sound.

Rabbit glanced over from where she was pulling out
long lengths of yellow silk from a compartment in the
floor, banners that were designed to show when the emperor was in residence. As far as Chih knew, no emperor
had ever come to Thriving Fortune.

"Do you play?"

"Who in the empire doesn't? My mother put the dice in my hand on my fifth New Year. The board was paper and the dice only stone, but it was the same."

"I wondered more if your vows prevent it, but here."

Rabbit came to kneel across from Chih, passing them a handful of pebbles. "Go on."

After a moment, Chih placed all of their pebbles on the lady, elegant, smiling, and dressed in the clothing of the doomed Ku Dynasty. Rabbit pulled up her sleeve to reveal a ropy scarred arm, and she shook the cup high and low before tumbling out the dice with an exhalation of "dah!" like a professional dealer.

The dice tumbled across the board, coming up fish, ship, and moon.

"Ah, unlucky," Rabbit said, sweeping the pebbles towards her. "You should never put all your money on one thing."

"I like doing it my way," Chih said with a smile and a shrug. "Was that how the empress played as well?"

"The empress . . . Well. She first saw the game after she had been living in the women's quarters for almost a month."

~

The new empress was like a ghost. At first, we were all

afraid of her, because the women of the north were all thought to be witches and sorceresses. Then they discovered her great secret, that she was only a heartbroken and lonely girl, and she became of no account at all.

There were almost three dozen accessory wives in the women's quarters at that time, but the most important by far was Kaofan, the daughter of the Kang clan of the east. Until she was banished south to live with the gravestone cutters and charcoal burners, she was more the empress than the empress, and she loved to play Moon Lady Ship.

One day, in the Chrysanthemum Room, where all the paper screens are filigreed with pale orange chrysanthemum petals, they were playing just as we played now, and Kaofan sat with one sleeve off her shoulder like a dealer in the water and flower district.

I was there, mending a robe that had torn along the sleeve, and so I noticed the empress just a few seconds before Kaofan did.

She stood in the doorway, her head tilted and her hands dangling by her sides. Her hair had been brushed and braided because the emperor had roared he was tired of seeing it in tangles, and there were great dark circles under her eyes.

"What are you playing?"

I am not sure any of us had heard her speak before this. Her voice was soft and deep, and it felt as if it came from a great distance away. For a moment, I was afraid that Kao-fan would be cruel to her, as she so often was to the junior wives, but instead she smiled.

"Come here, and I'll show you."

She explained the game to the new empress with exaggerated courtesy, sending sly glances to her especial friends. She showed her how the pictures matched the images on the dice and how to place her stake on each picture.

"What are we playing for?" asked the empress.

"Oh, we were playing for jeweled buttons, but if you don't have a stake . . ."

Silently, her face as still as a pond, the empress reached in her pocket to pull out buttons of jade set in jet. They were obviously of imperial make, and we were all reminded that whatsoever she chose to do with them, she was still the empress.

Do I need to tell you she won? It's not a game of skill, not really. That's why we teach it to little children at New Year's, to give them a taste for winning and to give the old gamblers a reminder that they are, after all, only mortal. She won, and won, and won, and in the end, she had a small mountain of jeweled buttons in front of her, and Kaofan had empty hands.

"I'll give these all back to you," she said after a meditative moment, "if you tell me where you got this board from."

Kaofan smiled, and In-yo dropped a fortune back into her hands as if they were no more valuable than pebbles she'd picked up off the street.

"There's a woman who comes with games sometimes. She travels up and down the coast to bring us back entertainment and games and fortunes. Would you like to see another game she brought us?"

In-yo looked at her, and when I look back, I still cannot tell what she saw when she looked at the most beautiful of all the emperor's wives. I wonder if she looked ahead to when Kaofan would end her life covered in charcoal and grit, or whether she saw the contempt that Kaofan had for her, and yes, even then, some of the fear as well.

I know very well, though, that In-yo never hated Kaofan. She may have pitied her, or been angry with her, or simply found her irritating or foolish or unfashionable. Hate, however, was reserved for equals, and as far as In-yo was concerned, she had no equals in all the empire.

Do you understand?

~

Chih thought for a moment before shaking their head.

"I think I come a little closer, grandmother, but no. I do not understand. Not yet."

Rabbit smiled, showing off her strong, sharp teeth.

"You are clever, aren't you?"

"So the clerics always thought, grandmother."

"Good. That is a good thing."

She went back to reeling out the yellow silk from the subfloor compartments and said nothing else that day.

Chapter Four

Bag of lychee fruit. Linen, ink, and lychee. Marked with a
weight of 10 tan and a regional stamp for Ue County.
Bag of hazelnuts. Linen, ink, and whole hazelnuts.
Marked with a weight of 10 tan and a regional stamp
from Tsu.
Plum-sized mammoth. Gold, rubies, enamel, and iron.
The mammoth is worked realistically rather than figu-
ratively, every hair detailed and with rubies serving as
eyes. The mammoth is caparisoned in blue enamel,
and the mammoth's tusks are capped with iron.

The magery that had locked down the entire region around Lake Scarlet for fifty years had kept Thriving Fortune's larder fresh. As they turned the golden mammoth over in their hand, Chih swiped a handful of lychee fruit from the bag. When they broke the paper-thin rind with their teeth, their mouth flooded with ridiculously sweet juice, a taste now more rare than rare with Ue County having declared sovereignty and closed its borders.

"That's too fine for the likes of you," Almost Brilliant

sniffed, but she did not turn away when Chih peeled two of the fruit and set them on the ground next to her. As the hoopoe ate, Chih went to find Rabbit, who was brewing a cup of herbal tea.

"Oh, why, I've not seen that in years. We thought it lost."

Her mouth was soft as she turned the mammoth over in her hands. It was the symbol of the northern people as the lion was the symbol of the empire of Anh. All their life, Chih had seen the mammoth and the lion together. The twinned beasts stared out from the carvings and crests with a kind of weary patience. They had seen empires rise and fall, they seemed to say, and they would see this one do the same.

Rabbit turned the mammoth upside down to show Chih what they had missed, a tiny maker's mark stamped on one round foot. Chih squinted to read it, peripherally aware of Almost Brilliant fluttering into the room and nesting overhead in the rafters.

"The characters for . . . *elegant woman* and . . . *civet cat*?"

"Yes. It is the professional chop of Yan Lian, the great artist. She went to live as a nun at the Phan Kwai abbey, but she was once quite the favorite in the capital."

~

The women's quarters were decked in fertile black and lucky red. The court physician had confirmed that the empress was with child. The court women wondered how In-yo could tell, so stocky and round, but they walked more carefully around her. Those who bear children hold the keys to life and death, and their ill wishes are to be feared.

After the announcement, the empress seemed to grow obsessed with fortune-telling of all kinds. She summoned fortune-tellers from town, from the borders, from faraway Ning and warlike Zhu. She entertained men who threw stones, women who dealt cards, even a person who was neither who had a horse that could tap out a number associated with the great holy book of the veiled peoples of the south.

I was just returned from escorting a mystic from the west back to the gates when a messenger arrived just ahead of me.

"The Emperor of Pine and Steel would honor you for housing the future prince."

He presented her with a package wrapped in silk, and she frowned when it came to light. It was a tablet of gold, soft enough to mark with a fingernail, heavy enough to thump against her chest if she wore it suspended from the gold chain it had come with.

I saw a brief flicker of dislike pass over her face even

as she thanked the emperor through the messenger. I turned to go as well, but she stopped me.

"Tell me, would you wear this?"

I mouthed the usual protestations, that I would be found for a thief and executed if such a thing ever sat on my filthy neck, but she shook her head.

"Tell me the truth."

"No, I do not like chains around my neck."

"Neither do I. Now tell me, girl, who is the finest artist you know?"

I should have said Chang Hai or someone like that, someone well-known at court for their flowers and their carefully sculpted peaches. Instead, I was so startled that I told her the truth.

When she answered the imperial summons, Yan Lian seemed to me as tall as a tree and as wild as the boar that roamed the forests near the capital. Her hair was cropped close to her head like a nun's, but she'd cut strange patterns into it, like sheared velvet, and her eyes were as narrow as her smile was wide. She wore men's clothes in those days, and she swaggered into the women's quarters as if everything in the world could be hers if she simply reached out and took it.

Yan Lian weighed the golden tablet in her hand, and she spilled the chain through her fingers like water. She nodded when she could mark it with her fingernail, and turned back to the empress.

"I can make you something beautiful with this gold, but surely, Empress, you know that nothing comes for *free*."

The wild artist put a special emphasis on the word *free*. I couldn't know it then, and the empress certainly didn't, but Yan Lian used the accent they use down in the water and flower districts, where every sensual pleasure commands a price and nothing is more embarrassing than getting a kiss for free, as if it were charity.

The empress may not have known what Yan Lian was implying, but she heard something in the other woman's voice and smiled.

"Come sit with me in my chambers. We have many designs to discuss. You, girl. What's your name?"

"Rabbit, great empress."

"Well, then, Rabbit, come here and sit in front of the door to my quarters. Stay there and keep any eavesdroppers well away. I should not like to see my designs copied."

I assume that at some point they spoke of designs. At least the little gold mammoth is caparisoned the way the imperial mammoths are for war. I do not remember designs, though. I remember laughing, and sighing, maybe some crying, or perhaps it was only moans that grew more desperate as the night went on. I remember one indignant cry of pain that dissolved into giggles, and the slide of skin on silk and skin on wood. Some of my friends from the kitchens sneaked me some rice and pickles before scampering away. I ate the food gratefully, but I barely tasted it, intent instead on listening to the empress and the artist at their work.

When dawn came, and I was just beginning to nod at my post, the door slid open. It was indecorous of me, but I glanced back into the empress's chambers to see her sprawled on her back, half-covered with a stained robe, her dark hair an inky spill around her head. She snored slightly, but it was a satisfied sound, and Yan Lian shook her head. There was a vivid red bite on her shoulder that she thumbed absently before she pulled her robe up to cover it.

"I've had magistrates and bandits, courtesans and opera singers, but rabbit-toothed girl, I have never had anyone like that."

Maybe she said it about every man and woman she bedded, but I think there was something genuinely awed in her voice.

Later on, when I brought In-yo her bathwater and perfume for her toilette, she told me to stay with her while she bathed. I watched as she rinsed her strong limbs, her dark skin coming up gleaming from the water. She was as little like a proper Anh lady as a wolf is like a lapdog, and when I caught her watching me out of the corner of her eye, I sat up very straight indeed.

"I saw you that first day, didn't I? You were the one who raised her face to me as I walked by."

I nodded, and then said timidly, "I had not seen that you noticed, Your Majesty."

She grinned at me, wrinkling her nose a little as she did so.

"They teach us to look out of the corners of our eyes when we are very young in the north. Less movement to startle the things we hunt or to attract the attention of those who would hunt us. What did you see when you looked at me?"

I thought about my answer carefully as I toweled her dry, spreading her cloak of black hair over a woolen cloth.

"I thought that you looked very strange to my eye," I said finally. "And very alone."

"I am alone," she said, tying her robe herself. "But maybe I am less alone than I thought I was, hmm, Rabbit?"

I blushed and ducked my head, murmuring something about duty and being honored to serve, but deep down, I thought she would never be alone again, not if I could help it. Being close to her was like being warmed by a bonfire, and I had been cold for a long time.

Whatever deal they struck, two weeks later a little

golden mammoth was returned to the palace wrapped in a twist of common cotton. In-yo looked at it and smiled, and I swear I had never seen anything so lovely.

~

Chih tilted their head to one side.

"Are you going to ask me if I understand? I am still not sure if I do."

"Well, something like this, you understand or you won't."

Chapter Five

Broken broom with tin charms tied around the handle.
Broken makeup compact. Alabaster, grease, and carmine.
Birch bark scroll. Birch bark, black feather, lock of hair,
and blue silk thread. The birch bark is rolled around
the hair and the feather, and tied together with the
thread.

Chih jumped when Rabbit came and took the birch bark scroll away from them, holding it in her hand as if she wanted to crush it.

"I will not ask if you understand this one, either, because if you were not born and raised in the Palace of Gleaming Light, you would not. In those days you could say a thousand things with your choice of ink and paper even before someone read a word of your poetry."

Chih looked at the object in Rabbit's hand, wondering why the hair and dark feather looked suddenly so grim.

"I thought it was just trash."

"It is trash," she said shortly, "but if you want to understand people who have gone, that's what you look at, isn't it? Their offal. Their leavings."

Chih waited patiently. It was the bulk of their training, learning how to wait for a story rather than chasing after it, and soon enough, it came to them.

Rabbit sighed.

~

This came to her door after she gave birth to the imperial prince, who was Kau-tan, known as the prince in exile. They'd taken him against her wishes, to wash him, they said, but she cried exhausted tears, knowing well she might never see him again.

I'd washed and bathed her, and after they took the little prince from her arms, I crawled into the bed with her, holding her and comforting her as best I could. There is nothing that can comfort a mother whose child was taken so unwillingly from her arms, though, and after the first sound of grief, she never made another. Instead, she asked me to tell her stories of where I had come from, my people, and I reached into the depths of my memory to tell her about living in the inn, how my father cooked enormous pots of barley stew for the people passing by, and my mother had read the fortunes of the great and the small alike between her chores.

The ladies of the women's quarters left us alone in the

dark, and so we lay together, skin to skin, for almost two weeks as she healed and I told her about my life out of the palace. It did not matter that it was so humble; what mattered was that it was outside the palace gates, and that was what she craved most.

This came for her from the emperor's own hand, much as you see it now. Strange how some trash survives, but precious things are lost, isn't it?

I sat with her and showed it to her, and when she wondered why her husband would send her trash, I explained it to her, wishing that the sky would open up and swallow me.

The hair belonged to her mother. It was as long as hers was and sleek black threaded with iron, known as well to her as the smell of snow waiting in the sky and the taste of seal meat. Seeing it here and wrapped in birch bark, the empress knew her mother was dead.

The jacana feather was a sign of exile, hers. She was lucky it was not a shred of willow bark, which would have meant execution.

The emperor had his heir from the north. He no longer needed a northern wife.

When I explained it to her, she went silent and turned her face to the wall, still as the sky before a lightning strike.

~

Chih waited to make sure that Rabbit was done, and then they nodded.

"I think I understand this, grandmother."

"Do you, cleric from the Singing Hills? Because I am not sure I wish to."

Rabbit was still, almost shaking with an emotion that had lived underground for a long time.

Gently, slightly nervously, Chih rested their hand on the woman's shoulder. They were faintly surprised to find Rabbit to be truly flesh and blood, and not the cold, misty dampness of a revenant.

"It is trash, and where I come from, we burn trash."

Rabbit looked startled, and then she nodded.

"Yes. We do that here as well."

That night, the smoke from their fire curled up into the wide sky, like the incense from a temple sacrifice. When they went to sleep, Chih dreamed of a woman in a beautiful tunic made of seal fur, iron threaded through her black hair. From the ice gates of the north, she looked south, unblinking, waiting for her daughter to return home.

Chapter Six

A day later, Rabbit came and laid a single vivid green leaf in Chih's hand. For a moment, Chih was startled to see a green leaf so far out of season, but then they saw that it had been dipped in wax, preserved for a season, a year, fifty years, or more with its bright color.

"Grandmother, what is this?"

"She asked me to get it for her as she lay on the palanquin that carried her west, which her people and ours have always said was the direction of death and endings. She'd listened to my stories, and she asked me if I would go with her into exile. As she said, at least someone would be able to go home again."

Rabbit paused.

"Of course because she was who she is, because she said that, I never wanted to go home at all. They were the people who gave me away to make up for the lack of five caskets of orange dye. I came to Thriving Fortune with her."

"Do you remember much of that journey, grandmother?"

"She was weak. So weak after what the doctors had done to her to prevent there ever being another heir to contest the rule of the first. But when she could, she rode with the curtains of her palanquin open, her face turned not west towards death or east towards civilization, but instead to the north."

"To home."

"Perhaps."

Chapter Seven

Box of cumin. Wood, copper, and spice.
Box of dried coriander. Wood, copper, and spice.
Box of black salt. Wood, copper, and spice.

"Cleric, when you were a child, did you ever play eagle-eye with your parents?"

Chih had grown somewhat accustomed to Rabbit's silent approaches. They were less supernatural, Chih decided, than imbued with a lifetime of habit gained of perfect service in a place where anything less could be punished by death.

"I don't believe so, grandmother. What is that?"

"It was something they did in the servants' quarters to teach us to see not only sharply, but well. They would fill a box full of small items, and then cover it. For one brief moment, they would unveil the items, and then cover them again. For every item you could remember, you'd get a sweet."

"We played something similar at the abbey for much the same purpose. Why do you bring that up now, grandmother?"

Rabbit pointed to the boxes of spices Chih had found at the rear of the pantry, half-covered with a gaily dyed cloth and unremarkable in every way. Since the north had come south, black salt was almost as common as white now, and considered far more beautiful.

"Because one of these boxes is no kin to any of the others."

~

Four years.

Four years we lived at Thriving Fortune with a revolving cadre of beautiful spies from the city. In-yo stayed in the empress's chambers closest to the lake waters, and I slept in the closet off the kitchen. The ladies who were sent to us from the Palace of Gleaming Light were out of favor, I believe. Less fashionable, less lovely, perhaps simply less lucky.

They came here with smiles and vows to serve, and they were always playing eagle-eye, watching for the slightest hint of treason, the slightest hint of impropriety that they could report back to court, winning a place in a vaunted company of betrayers and murderers.

Some stayed a season, and some stayed for almost a

year, but eventually, the Minister of the Left would arrive on his blood bay stallion, dressed in his favorite red and gold silk robe, embroidered with the figure of the noble kirin. He came to collect the previous ladies and to bring the new lot.

"It is far too much of a temptation for ladies to grow overfamiliar with their empress, especially in this desolate place," he explained in his calm and matter-of-fact voice.

"It does not do to have them grow to love me or to be too loyal to me, either," said In-yo.

She hadn't bothered to change out of her dressing robe to greet the Minister of the Left. He saw it as a sign of her uncouth slovenliness. I knew it to be a sign of her contempt. He smiled a smile as thin as a zither string.

"As you will, great and beautiful lady."

The new ladies, girls, really, giggled at his compliment, and they tumbled over themselves swearing to serve the empress faithfully and well. In-yo ignored then, and I did as well. If the Minister of the Left had ever thought that the empress would lower herself to befriend a simple servant girl, he would have found me guilty of all the overfamiliarity he pretended to worry about. I'd stopped learning the ladies' names sometime after the second year.

They were harmless, really. There was nothing for them to tease out. Sixty years of warmth and the hot winds summoned up by the imperial war mages kept the winter at bay, and without winter the mammoths of the north were dull and helpless, inclined to die of strange southern fevers and heartsickness.

Some of those girls, I think, might have come to love the empress in their own time. I do not remember love from them, however, so much as ambition. They'd ridden high once and then fallen, or perhaps they'd only seen the high places and it made them hungrier.

Kazu, I am convinced, must have been an accident. She arrived at Thriving Fortune with a slightly confused look that she never lost, and when the two other girls she came with knocked their silly heads on the ground trying to outdo each other in their obsequies to the empress, Kazu was more interested in the house, the woods around us, and the lake.

It turned out that she was one of the emperor's less successful whims, a beautiful inn girl plucked from the low city and elevated to the rank of an accessory wife. She should have gained glamour like a pearl gained nacre, becoming more beautiful, more refined. Instead, her most august setting only made her seem cruder, a paste gem in a setting of gold filigree.

Now, you must not think that I disliked her.

The first week Kazu lived at Thriving Fortune, she lay in bed and sulked, but she quickly grew bored with that. She learned very quickly that the other two ladies held no interest for her, and that left In-yo and me.

I was just sweeping the floor outside of In-yo's room when Kazu scared the wits out of me by catching the edge of the porch and hauling herself up from the ground.

"Don't do that! I thought you were some kind of wood spirit." I scolded her as if I were her big sister, speaking before I thought. She would have been well within her rights to slap me, but instead she grinned.

"It's boring here. Come on, I'll teach you a game, and we can play together."

"You can do what you like, but I am not going anywhere until I've cleaned this floor."

Kazu always struck me as more than a little lazy, but she could stand boredom far less well than she could stand work. She stripped out of her robes, right down to her trousers, and she came to clean next to me.

When we were finally done, she came to sit at the low table in the kitchen and taught me Lo-Ha, which was a dice game that was very popular in the capital that year. It relies more on luck than on skill, and in short order, I was nearly as good as she was.

It was addictive, however, and I ran off to play with

Kazu so often that In-yo came looking for me. I scrambled to my feet, humiliated to be caught idling, and Kazu wore the hangdog look of someone caught in the wrong, but unashamed of it.

"What in the world are you doing?"

And so Kazu taught Lo-Ha to the empress, who mastered it as she did all games of chance, with both skill and a nearly astonishing amount of luck. When she had beaten both of us roundly, she gave us an impatient look.

"Is this all there is?"

Kazu looked slightly affronted.

"Well, no. This is just for fun, right? People use this game for fortune-telling in the capital. When you throw a two, a five, and a seven like this, they look it up and they can tell your future. It's not just a game for children."

"It's definitely a game for children," In-yo declared, and then she narrowed her eyes.

"Do you have friends in the capital who know how to tell what fortunes you throw? Good ones, not cheaters and fakes."

Kazu snorted. "All fortune-tellers are cheaters, but maybe I know some good ones."

"They're not. Fortune-tellers have the ears of the gods. They tell us about the world we cannot see."

I heard a shushing step in the hallway, one of the other ladies shuffling away. Doubtless she was going to laugh at the empress's simple faith in festival fortune-tellers. The court fortune-tellers were a different breed entirely, of course, with well-fed bellies and sleek robes of cool green. It was easy to believe that they might have an eye on the doings of the gods when they had risen so far in the world. A poor barefoot fortune-teller from the market, well, that was perhaps a harder sell.

In-yo picked up one of the dice again, tumbling it between her fingertips. I knew that something was sizzling in her brain, burning away like a bonfire, but she only nodded at the table.

"Come on, play with me some more. I'm not tired of winning yet."

Every year, the north sent her a box of white salt. It gleamed like starlight, each grain perfect and clean. They sealed the boxes with wax so that the salt arrived as perfect as the day they harvested it from the sea.

In-yo had her secrets, sealed away inside her like a box with another box inside it and another inside that. Even as well as I knew her by the end, there was no end to the depths of her or the secrets she hoarded like a miser his chains of gold coins. I have no idea how she passed more than the faintest pleasantries with the north at that point, when all of her messages were scrutinized for codes, for invisible ink and pinprick holes that could spell out a message of rebellion.

All I know is that that year, the year that Kazu came to live with us, the year that we learned Lo-Ha, and taroco, and all the others, the north finally sent their exiled princess a box of black salt instead of white.

Do you understand?

~

Chih set the box of black salt on the table in front of them. After a slight nod from Rabbit, they opened the box again, looking at the black granules more closely. Almost Brilliant fluttered down from the rafter to inspect the box and the contents, pecking at the grains that Chih dabbed with a fingertip.

The grains of salt, they realized, were not really black, but instead a deep and dull garnet. When they bent their head down, they could smell a faint scent of spoiled milk and something underneath, something almost bloody.

"It's iron," they said with faint surprise. "Iron gives black salt its color, then?"

Rabbit nodded with some satisfaction. "It is. White salt is pure and comes from the sea, utterly innocent and utterly still."

"And red from iron, from swords and shields and the bells that hang from the mammoths' bridles . . . I imagine that black salt stands for something else."

"Yes. You do understand."

Chapter Eight

*Astrological chart of the constellation of the Baker. Fine
rag paper and ink. Signed in the lower-right corner
with the character for "lucky."*

*Astrological chart of the constellation of the Crying
Widow. Fine rag paper and ink. Signed in the lower-
right corner with the character for "mourning."*

*Astrological chart of the constellation of the Rooster. Fine
rag paper and ink. Signed in the lower-right corner
with the character for "open-eyed."*

Chih had thought the rear room to be a simple storage
room at first. They had not expected to slide open the
door and to be confronted with stacks of star charts filed
into glass-fronted cabinets, indexed with a dab of dye in
one corner and kept as carefully as the great scrolls of the
abbey in Singing Hills.

Above them, Almost Brilliant whistled, though
whether the sound was meant to be surprised or taunting
Chih could not guess.

"Well, this is certainly a mess."

"I suppose it is."

"Do you think you can get through all of them fast enough to get to the eclipse?"

Chih bit their lip. It would be a close thing. They worked fast, but after a certain point, speed became the enemy of precision. Precision was the watchword of the clerics who had raised them, but the tug of the capital and the eclipse over the Palace of Gleaming Light was powerful.

Finally, they shrugged, going to the topmost shelf on the right and pulling out paper, inkstone, ink, and brush again.

"This could take all month," Almost Brilliant said, alighting on their shoulder. Chih absently brushed the hoopoe off, ignoring the soft squawk of offense.

"It could. I hope it won't."

It would be, not appropriate, perhaps, but understandable to move on, to list the general contents of the room and to continue with the cataloging of Thriving Fortune. Another cleric could be sent, or perhaps Chih themselves could return at some point. By then, however, looters might have moved in and, as Chih listened to Rabbit's footsteps shushing somewhere through the compound, things might be very different.

Empress In-yo, dead precisely a year before the upcoming eclipse, was one of the most well-recorded monarchs in history. She had brought the clerics of Singing Hills back from their exile beyond the borders of Anh, and she personally gifted them a gorgeous ivory and brass aviary to nest the next generation of neixin. Then she had shut off every record of herself before her ascension, every place she had lived between her banishment from court and her return six years later.

The clerics of the Singing Hills never liked gaps in their knowledge, but in return for their lands and their restored place in Anh, they had let it go. Eventually, the historian clerics knew, things would come out, whether it took five years, fifty, or a hundred.

If Chih did not finish their work here, they knew with the slow patience of seven hundred years' worth of records at the abbey that it would be finished someday.

But I think this needs to be finished now. Soon.

The star charts ranged in quality from simple market scratches on elderly trash paper to beautifully elegant scrolls that described the heavens and their effect on those below in intense detail. Chih took a second glance at the ones related to their own birth sign, the Spoon, and was variously amused and impatient by turns to find predictions of varying accuracy. They had indeed come far from where they began in the foothills of Wa-xui, but they were hardly going to be called demure, maidenly, or docile.

A prickling along their back made them look up, and they turned to see Rabbit kneeling in the doorway behind them. She was not kneeling as if she were a dedicated servant waiting for orders, but instead, she knelt as if her legs would no longer support her, one hand on the door's edge, the other fisted on her knee.

"Grandmother! Did you fall?"

Chih came over to help the old woman up, but she pushed Chih aside, coming into the room to sit with the star charts and the slips of astrological fortunes.

"Grandmother?"

"Have you seen the secret yet?"

"No, not yet, grandmother. I see a great many fortunes. I see as many stars as there are in the sky, but I do not see the secret yet."

They thought Rabbit would tell them another story, but instead she merely pulled out two star charts. The first one Chih recognized from a famous old text that was part and parcel of every village fortune-teller's tool kit. She opened it to the constellation of the Rabbit, and then she pulled down another chart, one that Chih had already noted, passing the ball of her thumb over the signature in the corner, the character for *lucky*.

"Now play eagle-eye and look closely."

Chih did as they were bid, and after a few moments, they thought they had it.

"They are different. There are fewer stars in the newer chart, and even the ones that are meant to be there are shifted perhaps? Or twisted?"

Rabbit laughed hollowly. "Yes. The ones marked like this, they are wrong, or perhaps they are poorly made or made by fools. It is perfect, is it not? Who thinks that a village fortune-teller will have perfect sources? There are so many jokes about them making up the placement and the movement of the stars already."

Chih looked at the altered star chart more carefully, and as they did, they thought they could see a rhythm in the seeming carelessness and chaos.

"A code," Rabbit said. "A nearly invisible way to get information through the countryside when all of Anh knew that she was mad for oracles and fortune-tellers. Everyone knew that she talked to them all, the great and the mediocre and the frankly bad alike. It was a joke in the capital. The empress will not get out of bed unless a fortune-teller reassures her that it is all right to do so."

She paused for a moment, shaking her head.

"In all fairness, she did a great deal of business from her bed, still in her nightclothes. In-yo used to say that if she were going to be doing this kind of business, she might as well be comfortable."

Chih touched the altered star chart, looking at the off-set stars, the missing planets, and a star road that arched in a curve that was foreign to them. If they had run into it in the market, they would have said it was a singularly poor example of the astrologer's art, a pretty picture at best, and trash at worst. With Rabbit's explanation, it became something altogether other.

Their fingers brushed over the character in the corner, and Rabbit almost flinched.

"Lucky?"

"He wasn't, unfortunately." Rabbit's words were clipped as though with a seamstress's scissors. She pointed to a small volume half-hidden on the lowest shelf. It sat in shadow, and Chih wouldn't have noticed it until they got there.

"That's the catalog. You may choose to use it instead of marking down each of the charts yourself. It will save you some time, at any rate."

Chih opened their mouth to thank her, but Rabbit shuffled quickly out the door, sliding it closed behind her.

"Lucky," they repeated, and then they shivered.

Bad luck, during the reign of the last emperor, could be very bad indeed.

~

I missed Kazu after she was sent back to the Palace of

Gleaming Light. I didn't think I would. She was noisy and lazy and always more interested in fun than she was in anything like work, but she livened up the days, and at night she could be convinced to tell the bawdy stories that she learned from the rough men at the inns. You laughed with Kazu around, sometimes because she was so insolent, sometimes because she was so lazy, but most often because she was so much fun.

She was the only girl who ever cried when the Minister of the Left returned to bring her back to the palace, and when she asked to stay, he frowned at her, his mouth turning into the slash of a sharp knife through scraped hide.

"Of course your love for the empress does you credit. Perhaps in a year or two, when you may be spared from court."

I felt a cold and heavy stone settle in my stomach at his words, but Kazu brightened up considerably.

"Well, a year or so, that's not so bad. Then I'll be back and I'll have all sorts of games to play from the capital, won't I, In-yo? Won't I, Rabbit?"

"Oh, you *stupid girl,* I can't stand to hear your prattling."

In-yo turned impatiently to the Minister of the Left even as Kazu looked at her with hurt in her bright eyes.

"Do not send her back. She will not stop talking or

gaming, and you can be sure she did not do her chores."

The two other girls nodded wisely, and the two girls the Minister had brought to replace them with made quiet notes to themselves that the empress did not care for chatter. Kazu drooped like a poplar in drought, and even as In-yo turned around as if the matter bored her, I watched the Minister.

His eyes slid between the empress and Kazu and back again. I could see the grim math being worked there even if Kazu could not. Finally, he tucked his hands into his sleeves and nodded.

"I will endeavor to select better when next I am called upon to choose maidens for your home, my empress."

In-yo shrugged as if the entire matter was dull to her, and she never looked up to watch Kazu leave with the minister and the two other girls, whose names we had never bothered to learn.

Years later, In-yo tried to find Kazu, looking with both the chroniclers and the executioners, who kept their own secret records. Neither scholar nor killer could remember Kazu. There was a record of her in the registry of accessory wives when she first entered the Palace of Gleaming Light, and a record of her sojourn to Thriving Fortune and her return. After that, nothing.

The records close to the end of the emperor's reign were spotty and confused at best. It was easy to see how one humble and never very popular accessory wife could be lost. One night, In-yo and I became very drunk, and we talked about all the ways that Kazu might have escaped. She might have stolen away on a ship that went across the sea, or perhaps she was picked up by a passing god in disguise who could not resist her delighted laugh and her terrible luck at card games. Perhaps she had fallen in love with some intrepid maid or stableboy, and they had run off together, seeking fame and fortune on the frontier.

It didn't matter, of course. Whether she escaped or died, neither In-yo nor I ever saw her again.

She did make good on her word, however, despite how hurt she must have been by In-yo's farewell. A month after we saw the last of her, the fortune-tellers came to call. Some of them were true mystics and some of them were such terrible frauds that we took pity on them and found them work in the countryside. Some were looking for royal favor, and others were looking for fame. Out of the lot, we found three who became integral to In-yo's plans.

The oldest was Zhang Phuong, whose son had been killed by the imperial guards many years ago. Zhang's wife had turned herself into a kingfisher out of grief and fled the land, and now all he had to remember his wife by was a kingfisher tattoo on his neck, and all he had to remember his son by was the grief in his heart. He read the future in ivory tablets that clacked on the floor like broken teeth, and whichever you turned up would tell you which way to go.

The youngest was Wantai Mai, a girl from the south. She was an actress born from a gravestone cutter and a dove keeper, and I do not think she could have gotten more disreputable unless she actually did sport a fox's tail when she wasn't paying attention. She dyed her hair a bright peppery red, and she painted eyes over her eyelids, frightening me badly until I got used to her. She told me once that she had a nose for trouble, and that it hung off In-yo like the scent of fish off a fisherman. Mai would read a person's destiny in the lumps in their skull, scrubbing her stubby fingers through their hair and often at the same time surreptitiously feeling for their purse.

Between them was . . .

Ha, what shall I call him? In the missives, he was Lucky, though he was not. The first name that his mother gave him was after the fashion of their people, designed to make him invisible in the eyes of malevolent spirits. It was Bucket, and there was something truthful to it. He moved like a bucket on a rope, always on the verge of spilling all its water, tottering back and forth, faster than he intended to go. There was the name I called him, of course, but the habits of a lifetime die hard, and I do not wish that written down in any place where unfriendly eyes might see it.

When he was on assignment to the north, meeting with In-yo's oh-so-deadly relatives, they called him Sukai, after a kind of migratory bird. In-yo told me that the sukai spends four months of the year in her homeland, but of the other nine no one knows, so I will call him Sukai here as well.

Sukai lacked Mai's dashing and Phuong's dignity, but he had a gift for loyalty. I didn't know that the morning that he showed up, however. In-yo was in deep consultation with Phuong, and Mai was entertaining the two ladies-in-waiting, promising them fame and fortune and beauty that would echo through the ages.

I was peaceably scrubbing the floors outside In-yo's quarters again, listening with half an ear to her discussion with Phuong and keeping half an eye out for anyone who might choose to do the same.

Unlike Kazu, Sukai did not surprise me. Instead, he waved until he got my attention from the sand below, until I could not help but put my broom aside impatiently.

"What is it? Have you gotten lost down there?"

He grinned. He was not handsome, with a face that

looked a bit like a proper face had been made out of wax and then heated and pulled very gently askew. It was a good face, though, and I was already a little more sympathetic than my hard words suggested.

"No, sis, I've not gotten lost, but look at this."

I watched from the porch as he scooped up one of the rocks from the beach, and then another, and then another. They were pale in his dark hands, and then he threw them up in the air, one after another. I watched with skeptical interest as he juggled for me, but just as I was getting ready to return to my work, I realized there were not three stones, but instead five, and then seven, all without him stooping to pick up another.

You must not think that I am a credulous little fool from the provinces, for all that I was born out here. I had seen some of the finest entertainers the world had to offer during my short stint at court, and as smooth and skilled as Sukai was, I was far from impressed.

He seemed to sense this and, one after the other, he threw the stones he juggled with unerring speed and strength, sending them to strike the trees nearby with a sound like the cracking of the ice in spring.

He came down to three balls, then two, and then the last one he threw right at my face. I squawked, falling back because a good shot with a stone that size could have broken my nose or killed me. I moved back so fast,

I landed on my rear on the porch, eyes screwed up and afraid of the dreadful pain.

Instead of a stone striking me, however, I looked up to see a shower of peony petals falling down around me, pink and sweet.

Now Sukai levered himself up on the porch with a broad grin on his skewed face.

"Did you like that? I learned it from a woman who did magic in the low town, and she said it came from nature spirits—"

His words were cut off when in a rage I pushed him back off the porch. He landed with a thump on the soft ground below, but he stared up at me in shock. I must have been quite a terrible sight, my face still screwed up with fear and tears of panic and humiliation in my eyes.

"And now I have to sweep up all this mess! That was awful; don't do that again!"

I don't know what kind of response that would have gotten, whether he would have laughed at me or turned mean about how poorly I had taken his joke, but then we both became aware of the door behind me sliding open and In-yo striding out. She took in the scene at a glance, and glared down at the young man on the ground. Even as a young woman, In-yo had a tremendous glare, and Sukai scrambled to his feet, prepared, I suppose, to meet his doom like a man.

"Did you make this mess?"

"Your Majesty, yes, I did. Forgive me."

I honestly thought In-yo might simply snort and tell him not to do it again, but instead her eyes narrowed. She glanced at him, glanced at me, and then she pointed at Sukai.

"You will help her clean all of this up. And before you play your tricks, why don't you make sure that people will welcome them?"

"Yes, Your Majesty. Thank you for your mercy."

She did snort at that, and she went back into her quarters to look over dozens of star maps with Phuong. He was an especially skilled artist, and his maps were always perfectly scaled, perfectly up-to-date.

Sukai looked at me warily from the ground.

"May I come up?"

"She said you could, didn't she?"

"Yes, but that doesn't mean you said I could."

I waved him up impatiently, and then he startled me by taking the broom out of my hands.

"Here, sit on the rail, all right?"

I wouldn't. I went to sit with my back to the sliding door instead, but he was just as happy with that.

He swept up the peony petals, and as he did so, he danced with the broom, spinning it in his hands like a beautiful woman. As he did, he hummed a tune that was so jaunty that I couldn't help but tap my fingers on the porch, and then he grinned at me and started to sing about an angry rabbit who would not be amused no matter how funny a joke was.

"Or maybe you don't know what a funny joke is, did you think of that?"

He winked at me, as if I had given him the most splendid opening, and he started to tell me jokes, such terrible, terrible jokes, everything from the old one about the rabbit in the moon, to ones about the giant who pissed out the sea, to the dragon who became so drunk its thrashing spelled out the dirtiest joke in the world.

At first, I tried to keep my lips squeezed tight, because I do not think that kind of thing ought to be encouraged, but then my mouth started to tremble, and the laughter, never so much a presence in my life, bubbled up out of me, and I started to laugh.

Of course it encouraged him, and he started to tell even more ridiculous jokes, ones that made no sense at all, but I couldn't stop laughing, even to catch my breath.

When he finally stopped, my ribs hurt, In-yo and Phuong came out to see what was the matter, and all I could do was try to tell them why the idea of an elephant walking a tightrope wire was so very funny.

"Well, I am glad that someone is having a good time," she said, but there was a slight smile on her face as she said it.

~

Almost Brilliant cocked her head to one side, looking at Rabbit.

"I do not forget anything, you know."

Rabbit nodded.

"I know. But this cannot be counted like boxes of spice and star charts."

The hoopoe pecked idly at the grains of rice the old woman had brought her, as if buying herself some time to think.

"This will not be a secret. I will likely tell Chih when we are alone, and of course anyone who asks, as well as my chicks whenever I should have them."

Rabbit sighed, spreading her hands out as if she did not necessarily understand herself.

"That is fine. But let them ask, and perhaps let them be kind when they do so. Some things are easier to explain to the birds and the beasts of the forests than to even the most sympathetic of clerics. He was unimportant, the least of In-yo's spies and couriers, but—"

Almost Brilliant fluttered her wings in the dying light.

"I understand. I will remember Sukai for you, and so will my children and their children as well."

"Thank you."

Chapter Nine

Canister of marked flat sticks. Horn, silver, and wood.
The horn canister is bound with strips of fine inlaid
silver. The sticks inside are carved with runes from the
north.
Three bound sticks. Wood and leather. The sticks come
from the canister, pulled apart from the set and bound
with a thin leather cord.

Of course Thriving Fortune was haunted; most places in Anh were. The country had been Ahnfi hundreds of years ago, and before that Cang, and before that, lost except to the clerics of the Singing Hills, it was Pan'er, whose capital was drowned by the waves of an angry sea god.

Ghosts were part and parcel of life in Anh, more worrisome than rats, less worrisome than the warrior-locusts that swarmed out every twelve years. Chih did not fear ghosts, but, they thought, as they cataloged the possessions of the deceased empress, they might be afraid of becoming one in this lonely compound on the shores of Lake Scarlet.

Thriving Fortune had a certain kind of irresistible gravity. The more they studied the life in exile of Empress In-yo, the more they looked, the more they wanted to look. More often than not, they could feel Rabbit watching them from some corner or doorway, waiting patiently as they pulled out more and more of the story that she had lived.

That morning, they uncovered a carved box tucked behind a basket for laundry, and when they brought it to Rabbit, the old woman chuckled with a kind of malice.

"Oh yes. Those are called Lucky Sticks in the capital. They are of northern origin, written in T'lin runes. Unfashionable, of course, until In-yo sat the lion throne. I do not suppose you have ever seen them before?"

"No. When I go to record the eclipse, this will be my first time in the capital."

"Well, that sounds very fine. Here, let me show you how to play."

Chih sat down across from Rabbit on the porch and watched as the old woman capped the box and rattled the sticks packed inside. As she did so, she took on the droning cry of the market fortune-tellers.

"Here Xao Min, goddess of luck! Here Fei-wu, god of wealth! Here Shao Mu, saint of love! Look upon our hands with kindness, and guide us towards what is right!"

She gave the small container a little bounce in her

hand while at the same time turning it over and removing the cap. The sticks themselves were too tightly packed to all come out, but three slid forward partway. With a practiced hand, Rabbit whipped them free and spread them on the ground in front of Chih.

"I take it you do not know T'lin?"

"They started teaching it after I served my novitiate. Those who came after me knew it, but I've not had the time to take it up, personally."

"You should find the time. It will never replace Anh as the national writing, but it will only grow more common the more traders come from the north. Ah, but let's see what you have drawn. I see the rune for north, the rune for run, and the rune for ambergris."

As Chih watched, Rabbit dug two fingers into the canister, pulling out a fragile piece of paper folded into thirds. It was covered with an insectile script, and Rabbit squinted at it for a long moment before she nodded.

"See, this combination means that you will be successful in your career, but only if you remember to take things in their own time. No one likes a prodigy, after all. Patience should be your watchword."

"So my teachers have always said. Thank you for reading for me."

"Now show me you have the trick of it. Why don't you

try reading the fortune that was tucked where you found this one?"

Chih shrugged and rolled open the bundled sticks, some fortune drawn long ago. In another place, they might have been impatient with this, but after what they had already learned and from the way Rabbit was watching them—*teaching* them—there was something else to be gained here.

The sticks were slightly darker than the ones in the canister, as if they had been turned hand to hand over a long period of time. It took Chih a few moments to parse out the blocky T'lin script, so very different from the curving syllabary employed throughout most of Anh. Then they hunted the matching ideogram on the ancient piece of paper, careful not to crumple it in their fingers.

"I think . . . this must be the rune for wind, and this the rune for wool? And perhaps this one is the rune for water?"

"No, they're not. It's not eagle-eye this time. Listen instead, and remember that the back of the north was originally broken by the empire of Anh in the days of Emperor Sho. In those days . . ."

"They spoke the southern Anh dialect, not what we speak now."

Rabbit smiled. "Yes. They still teach the southern dialect to the clerics, don't they?"

"Yes. So in the southern dialect, let's see. Water. Wind. Wool. Water. Wool. Water. Wind . . . Ba. Ber, kon . . ."

"And that's the southern dialect. Now bring it back to the northern tongue."

Chih concentrated. Translate the syllabary from T'lin, and from there into the southern tongue, and then use those building blocks to create words. . . .

"Konshi . . . Erh Shi Ko. He was a general, wasn't it? The one who led the Anh troops at Ko-anam Fords."

"It was. Very good. In-yo insisted on sending her fortunes at Lucky Sticks back to her home for interpretation. Of course the Minister of the Left suspected espionage. It was, after all, his job. He never let her send the sticks themselves, but he had a scribe come down and copy the markings to send along. The fool never knew that it wasn't In-yo's language that doomed him, but his own, brought to the north generations ago."

Chih played with the sticks, sounding out the name of the so-called Iron General, Erh Shi Ko. He died in the first purge, and his head was torn from his body and stuck on a stake as he had once ordered for all the men he'd captured in the northern conflict.

The clerics of the Singing Hills were always aware of the risk of seeing too much. The burn marks on the abbey's thick stone walls spoke of many warlords and monarchs who did not wish to be seen so clearly, and then every few years an elder neixin, rich in wisdom and experience, was traded with the sibling-abbey in Tsu, where she could teach the foreign hatchlings all she knew.

Chih had grown up with the history of the world in the very walls of their home, fluttering above their head, cooked into the barley they ate. This was the first time they could feel such a weight of it pressing down on them, wrapping around them like a blanket of wet wool.

~

The cleric looks at Thriving Fortune and sees the history they own as a subject of the empire. As a member of their order, perhaps they own it twice over, and I do not begrudge them that. The Empress of Salt and Fortune belongs to all her subjects, and she was romantic and terrible and glamorous and sometimes all three at once. There are dozens of plays written about her, and some are good enough that they may last a little while even after she is gone. Older women wear their hair in braided crowns like she did, and because garnets were her favorite gem, they are everywhere in the capital.

In-yo belonged to Anh, but Thriving Fortune only belonged to us.

It was a prison at first, because it always was one, a

place where emperors could banish wives who no longer pleased. It was better than the executioners' silk garrote, at least, though the emperor's executioners could travel as well as anyone. There are some very elegant ghosts that walk the edge of the lake, their long hems fading into the bracken. Some of them have handmaidens following along behind them, tongueless, handless, and eyeless, and I knew very well what might come of my loyalty to In-yo.

Thriving Fortune was also a refuge, at least for me. At the palace, I scorned the countryside as much as any of the other girls, more, because I was always worried they could smell the mud on me. Now I could breathe the fresh air and eat food as it grew straight from the ground. In-yo laughed the spring day I pulled up a full basket of spring radishes, but she ate them as quickly as I did. They were so fresh and spicy and perfect that if I sit in the spring breeze, letting the wind touch my cheek, I can taste them still.

Finally, Thriving Fortune became a war camp, and the general sat on the porch late into the night, looking north towards home and east towards vengeance. She took reports from her fortune-teller spies, sometimes under the very noses of the court ladies the Minister of the Left had assigned. In her eyes, I could see the watching spirits of her dead kin, who would rather their women died than be sent south unless they went as weapons.

In-yo's two attendants were napping the hot summer morning that Sukai returned with a message from her northern fortune-teller. Sukai looked, to me, rather more grown-up than he had appeared the first day I met him, fuller in the face, more cautious in the way he held himself. It made him more attractive to me, but it wasn't as if he had started out ugly in the least.

"You've brought word from Igarsk-Ino? What did he say about my luck for the coming year? I sent him three fortunes to interpret."

The only thing that revealed In-yo's impatience was the Lucky Stick she twirled through her fingers. I was the only one who knew how often she played with that stick, marked with the northern rune for death, which requires no interpretation.

Sukai passed her the first slip that had been copied down for her. The characters stood for *coal, mountain,* and *spear,* chu, ma, and rho. Ma Chiroh was a beast of a man, one of the little generals who saw the colonies as his personal hunting ground whether he was hunting for seals, deer, or women.

"As to the first fortune, the holy man says that it is most fortuitous. Your worries will be laid to rest, and they will never rise again."

He never did. He disappeared on a hunting trip, and

some years after that, he was found with a woman's spindle in his eye, his clothes blowing like banners from his bones.

In-yo nodded with relief.

"That is very well-done. And the second?"

Sukai passed her the second scrap of paper, inscribed with the northern runes for hail, wheel, and south, or pah, lo, and tze. Po Lo-tsu was one of the imperial war mages who kept Anh in perpetual summer, a man of discipline and great dignity.

"Igarsk-Ino pondered over your second fortune for a very long time, Your Majesty, and at the very last, he said that your life requires caution and hope in equal measure. We may think that the sun will never rise at midnight, but it has been known to happen."

Po Lo-tsu turned out to be the sun who rose at midnight after all. When the time came, he did as the north asked. That is, he did nothing, and in the chaos and bloodshed that followed, I am given to understand that he closed himself off in his quarters. They found him with the tin scent of strong poison on his breath, and a miniature portrait of his daughter in his hand. His daughter was a great beauty, and she had gone into the women's quarters at the Palace of Gleaming Light many years ago, during the reign of the emperor's father. She disappeared like Kazu did, like any number of women did over the years, unremarked, and their demise as unremarkable as surely they were not. One drunken evening, many years on, In-yo would say that the war was won by silenced and nameless women, and it would be hard to argue with her.

That day, however, In-yo only nodded, leaning forward with her eyes narrowed.

"And the third? What of the third?"

It was shi, erh, and kon, the name of the general who had killed her brother, and when Sukai shook his head, In-yo clenched her fists so tightly that her nails cut into her palms.

"The great fortune-teller consulted the stars and the old books, Your Majesty, and at the end, he merely said that some endeavors are too great to be attempted. Some ambitions must be left to lie until one is strong enough to conquer them."

In-yo nodded as if she understood, but when it came to Erh Shi Kon, she did not want to conquer. She wanted nothing less than a slaughter. Instead, she thanked Sukai for his service, and asked him to stay for a little while so she might ponder over what she had learned. In-yo was very good at waiting, but that particular fortune she craved.

There were of course other messages to be sent and houses in the capital where Sukai could offer his services, houses where the topic of who sat the lion throne was less words written in stone than a fortune written on birch bark. However, it did not escape me that In-yo might have had another reason to keep Sukai at Thriving Fortune when she told me to take him hunting mushrooms early one morning.

"It is strange to see a shadow without the one who casts it."

I scowled at him, looking up from where I was inspecting the loam.

"What nonsense are you about now? You will scare off the mushrooms if you are not quiet."

He cocked his head at me curiously.

"Are you serious, or are you trying to get me to shut up?"

"Mostly the latter, unless you can speak some sense. Why are you speaking about shadows?"

"Because this is the first time I think I have seen you out of arm's reach of the empress."

"Because you have made a careful observation of all her movements and mine, and you know where we are at all times."

"Well, less hers than yours."

I felt a deep red blush come up on my cheeks and, unused to the sensation, I tried to rub it off.

"You are being foolish. And here, give me the basket."

I came up with two wrinkled mushrooms, dark and smelling of good earth. I showed Sukai how to pull them up without disturbing the loam, ensuring they would continue to grow the next year. He looked at them dubiously.

"These look terrible."

"You may give me your share if you like, though I'd guess you'd change your tune once we fry them in sesame oil."

"Now, I didn't say that. I merely said they look too ugly to be as delicious as the empress was saying."

"Sometimes . . . sometimes the ugliest things can be the most delicious."

I looked at him sideways as I said it, blushing even darker, and he stared at me.

"Did— Was that a compliment? Did you try to pay me a compliment? Have you never paid one before?"

"No!"

He laughed so loudly that if mushrooms could run, we never would have found another one. We filled the basket with the small wrinkled mushrooms that In-yo liked so much as well as an orange and red-lobed one that smelled impressively like chicken.

Sukai proved to be a little hopeless at mushrooms and more than a little hopeless at directions. He came so close to wandering off down the mountain that, finally, I took his hand to lead him all the way back.

Just because I didn't want to lose the mushrooms, of course.

That night, while the other two ladies slept, the three of us fried the mushrooms over a small brazier set up on the porch. It had been overly warm all month, and the lake glowed like a baleful eye, eerily beautiful.

"How do you live with it watching you?" asked Sukai, forgetting that he was with royalty.

In-yo, who seemed to forget that fact whenever it was convenient for her, shrugged.

"As you live with anything, I suspect. You bear it, or you end it. So far, we have proved equal to bearing it."

With my mouth stuffed full of mushroom, I didn't say that you could also find a beauty in it, a kind of peace even in something that was at first so very unsettling. I'd cried the first time I saw the luminescence of the lake. Now most nights, I slept on the porch, bathed in its red glow. If it was a monster of some kind, it was a monster that watched over me, and, at the very least, it had not devoured me yet.

I didn't say it that night, but I did tell Sukai about it eventually. By then he had lost his fear of the lake entirely, and I had lost my last reservations of him.

~

Chih didn't realize that Rabbit had actually left Thriving Fortune until they saw her return, coming up the paved path and brushing dirt off her hands. There were blots of ink all over her fingers, and her expression was oddly solemn.

"What have you been doing, grandmother, if I might ask?"

"You might ask, certainly. I have been burying some writing of mine."

Chih cocked their head to one side.

"You must know that there's nothing that is more anathema to Almost Brilliant and me."

"Which is why I waited until you and the neixin were occupied in the storage rooms, yes."

Chih waited, and Rabbit sighed.

"Time is the thing. I want time to get the words right. To do proper honor to those who died. I don't want them to be ashamed when others speak about them. But I know that there is only so much time left, and it will never be perfect."

Tentatively, Chih reached out their hand to Rabbit, who took it blindly.

"The abbey at Singing Hills would say that if a record cannot be perfect, it should at least be present. Better for it to exist than for it to be perfect and only in your mind."

Rabbit was silent long enough that Chih thought they

would not get a response, and then she nodded.

"You are right, I suppose. Tomorrow. I will compose my thoughts tonight, and tomorrow I will tell you more."

Chapter Ten

Tin shrine token, badger with one paw raised.
Wooden shrine token, cherry inscribed with the aphorism
  "Submission but only to the truth."
Pilgrimage Itinerary. Fine rag paper and ink. The itiner-
  ary lists twenty-four shrines throughout the empire of
  Anh, each with a check mark next to it.

The two dozen shrine tokens scattered across the low table where they worked made Chih think of toys or sewing notions. They were the simplest of souvenirs, sold by the clerics at each stop as minor blessings to make a little more money for a new roof or a statue. In Singing Hills, they sold a little perfumed wax figure of a perched hoopoe, and Chih noticed that there was no such token in with the rest.

There was something almost sinister about the tokens and the itinerary, and after Chih recorded them, they put their brush down. There was a weight to the tokens that went beyond what they were. Thriving Fortune itself seemed to be a place made of stories and plots, conspiracies and fury.

Finally, they scooped a handful of the tokens and went looking for Rabbit.

They found her at last on the beach. As Chih watched, she bent to scoop up a rock, inspecting it closely before throwing it towards the water. She tried twice, making a face both times before shrugging.

"Sukai could send them skipping across the surface, four, even five or six times. I have never gotten the trick of it."

"It helps, I think, to spin them a little and to send them out rather than up. What can you tell me about these?"

Rabbit did not look surprised at all when Chih presented her with the tokens. She did not take them from the cleric but instead picked through them with one finger like a child sorting out her favorite nuts from a mix.

"Well, that one came from shrine of the Dancing Girl. She's not a goddess anymore, not enough worshipers, but back then, she did all right. It provided a place for all the little girls orphaned by the fighting to the far west to go, anyway. And this, this one came from the abbey in Bangala, where the monks and nuns claim that it was a rabbit that taught them how to fight. I've still never seen anything move as fast as one of the Bangala nuns showing us how she could throw six kicks in the space of one breath, each one knocking a stacked piece of wood high into the air."

She paused, looking at Chih shrewdly.

"But you do not want travel stories."

"I want to know all of it, and I think it might begin with travel stories. If you speak, grandmother, I will listen."

Rabbit sighed, and Chih thought of the fairies that could do anything, if only they were asked with exactly the right words. Rabbit sat down on the beach, and after a moment, Chih sat down with them. During the day, the waters were a translucent flint green, as beautiful and unremarkable as any other lake. It took nightfall to show the truth.

~

In-yo's pilgrimage was a thing that took us nearly two years to arrange. It was perhaps the most Anh thing she had ever done, and while I am sure that there were people in the capital who were relieved that the foreign empress was falling in line, the Minister of the Left did not agree.

He appeared at Thriving Fortune one autumn day, as unannounced as it was possible for a man like that to travel. He made no pretense of being on some errand but instead appeared with his house guard and not so subtly demanded an audience.

"It is well done of you to walk in the footsteps of the

most holy among us, but perhaps it might be better considered of you to remain at home."

In-yo gazed at him beyond the beaded curtain that separated her seat on the elevated platform from the rest of the audience hall. She was, that day, the very picture of an Anh empress in exile, but I could tell that the Minister of the Left disliked it as much as he had any other greeting that she had given him.

"And why should I remain at home? Are the roads too dangerous for my palanquin to travel? Is there unrest in the capital?"

"Of course not. The emperor rules over the land of Anh with the will of the great gods themselves, and there is no such disorder in his house."

"Then why should I not visit the holy places of my adopted homeland, as Empress Lan-ti and Empress Dunian have done before me?"

She named two ancestresses of the current emperor, women renowned for their piety and docile natures, and the Minister of the Left's mouth thinned with displeasure.

"My empress, begging your pardon, but they both were born of Anh nobility. The empire sees you differently than they saw those empresses."

In-yo was silent behind her screen. Seated in my obscure corner of the hall, I could see a tiny twitch of movement, her hand tightening on the bulky silky robes that I had dressed her in that morning.

"Anh is my home now, Minister. If the people tear me to bits, then I suppose I was wrong to trust this land and the protection of the emperor."

The Minister of the Left could not argue with her. He could bully, he could imply, and he could outright lie, but in the end, she was the empress, a step away from divinity, and he was only a man. I could see him toying with the idea of simply posting his guard around Thriving Fortune, wondering what it would cost him, whether he could sustain it for only the vague suspicions he had of the foreign empress.

In the end, I suppose he reckoned that his attentions were better spent elsewhere, and after a few more suggestions that she might find the road too wearisome or risky, he rose to leave. As he did, however, he glanced over to the side, where the household staff knelt in attendance, and he saw Sukai.

"I know you, don't I, fortune-teller?"

"You do, my lord. I have read for the empress many times over the past few years."

"I see. And of course, you will not be accompanying the empress on this mission?"

"I am, my lord. The empress has said that she would like my insight when we reach the skies of the west."

The Minister turned back to In-yo.

"This is the man you send north to your barbaric oracles there, isn't he?"

"He is," she said, contriving to sound bored and impatient at once.

"There is something of a fashion for the northern arts in the capital right now. I wonder if I could borrow your man to come and entertain some of the women in my household."

In-yo shrugged.

"If you like. You have my itinerary, and you may send him along when you are done with him."

Sukai had no choice but to leave with the Minister's guard, and after they were off the property, In-yo turned to me with a sorrowful look in her eyes.

"You could have kept him with us," I said that night, brushing out her thick, wavy hair. I kept my voice softer than a whisper, so soft that the waver in it was ironed out almost completely.

"I could have, but it might have cost me something else. I am sorry."

When I stay up at night, sometimes I think she must have reckoned the cost cheap. She was able to go on pilgrimage, where we took in the scenery, had our fortunes told by some of the greatest fortune-tellers in the empire, and incidentally assessed the strength of the empire's weather mages, fortifications, and troops as well as their loyalty, and all it cost her was one fortune-teller.

I suppose it should have cost her my regard and my love as well. It might have, but as I moved to put the brush away, her hand came up to cover mine. She did not promise to make it up to me, because there was no such possibility, and she did not say that everything would be all right, because it never would be.

I had cast my lot in with In-yo long ago, however, maybe from the time she told me one of us should go home if we could. Her home was in the north, and mine rode east with the Minister of the Left, so we would have to do as best we could with each other.

It was a grand procession as we moved south and west from Thriving Fortune. An empress's pilgrimage is no small endeavor. Attendants, guards, support staff, and baggage bearers were all part of that long, slow train, and, of course, there were the enormous cages of doves.

That was another Anh tradition, of course. The empress would release doves along the way, delighting the populace with the flight of dozens of white birds. We did not have Sukai with us, who knew all the back roads of the country, but we did have Mai, who was a dove keeper's daughter. Into the great and cooing flock, she entered her own birds, bred to do one thing and one thing only. At every shrine along the way, one of her clever birds took to the air with the others released, and then it winged its way north, a message in code wrapped around its thin leg.

The first part of the trip, In-yo was in a temper. She sent away the drovers for the least infraction, and dismissed the cooks and attendants out of hand. They knew the royal treasury would pay them a severance fee, so they went quietly enough, and we had to hire more people along the way. The royal pilgrimage looked quite ragtag after a while, but we pressed onward, even as it seemed the drovers could barely steer the oxen and the cooks couldn't do more than burn mash.

Phuong's heart gave out when we crossed the lake where his wife had turned into a kingfisher. We stopped for half the day to bury him in his finest robes and with his pouch of ivory tablets in his hand. All year, he had run back and forth across the countryside for us, his dignity allowing him entry into the most elite celebrations and his age making him no threat to the young wives who wanted their fortunes read and perhaps had a little taste for treason. When we'd shed our tears and moved on, I glanced over my shoulder to see a kingfisher come to sit on his cairn.

At the shrine of Matulan the turtle god, Mai dragged me off to eat roast pork with her among the gravestones while In-yo was busy pretending to listen to the abbot speak of patience and piety. I didn't want to be among the tombs of Matulan's worshipers, but Mai was right at home, seating me in front of one post while taking another for herself.

"We're all alone here but for the dead. There's no need to be afraid," she said, passing me the leaf packet filled with pork in a sticky honey sauce. I nibbled at the charred parts, my favorites, and I watched red fireflies dance among the stones.

"I'm not afraid," I said. "Whatever happens now, fear is behind us, isn't it?"

Mai laughed at my bravado.

"Such a brave Rabbit! It is a shame about your man, but at least your baby will be courageous as a lion, thanks to the pair of you."

Her words struck me like a hammer blow. She was surprised that I didn't know. The women of her old acting troupe had all kept track of their monthly cycles with ruthless precision to prevent exactly this sort of surprise.

"But that's good, yes? A surprise for him if he comes back, a consolation if he does not."

I struck out at her blindly and furiously, and she let me box at her with increasingly feeble blows before finally tucking her shoulder under my arm and helping me back to my bed in the encampment.

"Save that anger," Mai said with a sigh. "Angry mothers

raise daughters fierce enough to fight wolves."

In-yo was surprised when I crept into her arms that night, but she wrapped herself around me like a blanket.

"Is there going to be a place for all of us in your world?" I whispered to her, still mindful of the wakeful ears around us.

She kissed the top of my head comfortingly, and I told her my secret. She listened calmly, and she wiped my eyes when I cried. It came to me that she held me tighter after that, more protectively, and I might have thought that even then her mind was skipping forward to what came next, if only she hadn't spoken to me the next day. As we rode on the palanquin, she asked Mai to play us a merry tune from the back of her ox. When she thought our words would be sufficiently drowned out, she turned to me.

"So, what do you want for your child? Or do you want a child at all?"

I didn't know. I had spoken bravely to Mai the night before, but inside I was sick with fear. In-yo listened to my stuttering response, and then she took my hand, making me look right in her eyes.

"I have taken everything from you. It is the nature of royalty, I am afraid, what we are bred for and what we are taught. I will not take more unless you tell me it's all right. Do you understand?"

I did. We rode onward, Mai releasing her birds at every stop along the journey, playing music for me when I grew tired or nauseated, sneaking out at night to bring us treats from the towns we passed.

She's still alive now, you know. Not long ago in the capital, I saw her in a festival crowd. She was completely unchanged, and she winked at me, one eye real, the other painted on her eyelid, before she disappeared into the crush. Maybe she was a fox girl after all, come to bedevil an empire when it was at its most fragile, or perhaps she only has a daughter.

The Minister of the Left remembered what In-yo had said about sending Sukai along when he was done with him. We were almost home, just finishing up at the shrine of the Brothers Lai, when a messenger appeared, stone-faced and with a large lidded leather bucket sealed with wax.

Mai dragged me away from that scene, and In-yo was the one who broke the seal and looked in. She sent the messenger away with a curse, and she and Mai came to sit with me.

I felt so very old. At less than twenty-five, before everything that came after, I had no idea how long life was. I sat with an empress on one side and a red-haired actress on the other, feeling their touch on my shoulders, my hair, and my face, their bodies close to mine.

As we sat on the bank above the river, the bells of the Brothers Lai softly chiming the sunset, I felt a chilly wind ruffle my hair. When I glanced up, it struck me that the leaves were browning at the edges, withering a little even as I looked.

~

"Well, cleric?"

"Grandmother?"

"What are you going to do with what you have learned here? You know where this ends, and if you don't, I will not think much of the teachings of the clerics of the Singing Hills."

It was Almost Brilliant who answered, whistling a few hollow notes even as she went to splash her feathers through the waves that lapped up towards their feet.

"Do you think this kind of information is new in Singing Hills's records? It is not. The information in our archives could topple every throne in the world."

Chih spoke more slowly.

"I think the real question is why you told it to us. You loved Empress In-yo."

"With all my heart. Sometimes I loved her more, and sometimes I loved her less, but yes."

"This information could tarnish her memory beyond

repair, unseat everything that she spent her life working for. And you are telling it to me, painful as it is for you. Why?"

"In-yo is gone now. So are Phuong, my parents, and Sukai. My allegiance lies with the dead, and no matter what the clerics say, the dead care for very little."

"And the new empress, who is even now preparing for her first Dragon Court?"

Rabbit smiled. "Angry mothers raise daughters fierce enough to fight wolves. I am not worried for her in the least."

Chapter Eleven

Painting of the rabbit in the moon. Silk, paint, and wood.
Against an indigo background, a rabbit curves inside
the silver moon.
Painting of the fox mother leaving her children. Silk,
paint, and wood. As in the old story, a woman with a
foxtail cries over her children as she prepares to leave
them forever.
Hanging box containing a robe. Silk, silk cord, metallic
thread, and wood. The red and gold robe, embroi-
dered with a large kirin along one side, has been
folded carefully and preserved inside the box. The box
is plain with a loop of silk cord fastened to one end,
meant to be hung or carried.

Chih looked at the robe, and then turned to Rabbit, who was sitting next to them expectantly.

"You have mentioned this robe before. The Minister of the Left wore it."

"He did. In-yo came from people with conquest in their blood just as much as the people of Anh have. All of us believe in trophies."

"Tell me the rest of it, grandmother?"

"Of course."

~

By the time we returned to Thriving Fortune, we could see our breath hanging in the cold air. The leaves had fallen from the trees, and the sun would not come out beyond her robe of clouds for shame.

Mai and I had never felt winter before, and it was terrifying and exhilarating at once. It felt as if the world was dying around us even as the air grew crisper and sharper than anything we had ever known.

With every step we took into the cooling world, In-yo's hair grew blacker and her eyes brighter. She woke up in the morning and breathed in great lungfuls of the cold air until she was almost drunk with it. She looked north, and her eyes shone with a viciously bright light.

One morning we came out of the inn to a dusting of snow on the ground and more falling down. It was the first snow in the Anh empire in almost sixty years, and as the people around us murmured with fear, In-yo started to laugh.

We returned to Thriving Fortune to find the Minister of the Left waiting for us with all his household guard.

We arrived at dusk, when the dying light gave his pale features a bloody cast. I thought of what In-yo had not allowed me to see in that sealed leather bucket, and I thought I would be sick.

From atop her palanquin, In-yo watched him as he ordered her surrounded. She was calm, the calmest person there.

"Well, Minister?"

"We have word of events taking place along the border that necessitate returning you to the capital for your own safety, Your Majesty. I and my household troops will escort you there."

In-yo looked around with exaggerated curiosity.

"What events are these that you speak of, Minister?"

"Do not play the innocent, Your Majesty. You know very well. And now you will come with me."

I realized that even then, the Minister of the Left thought he was in control. Even with the mammoth cavalry of the north crossing the Ko-anam Fords, even with troops following the mammoths at the Li-an pass, and assassins killing off the nobles who would not be swayed, he thought that the empire of Anh as it was would be preserved. After all, he had the trump, the most beloved daughter of the northern people, and even savage as they were, they would balk at seeing her hung from the walls of the Palace of Gleaming Light.

His men moved closer, spears held at the ready, ignoring the rustle that ran through the procession. What are drovers and cooks and baggage handlers to soldiers, after all?

Of course we were no longer traveling with drovers and cooks and baggage handlers at all. In-yo had replaced the procession with her own soldiers, come south to meet us, and suddenly it was the Minister and his men who were surrounded.

In-yo tilted her head slightly at him as his men threw down their weapons.

"I am, in fact, going to the capital very soon, but you will not be accompanying me."

If there was room in my heart for anything but a vicious hatred for the Minister of the Left, I might have been impressed by how calm he was. He watched his men surrender and move away from him, and he must have known that whatever happened to the Anh empire, it was the end for him. He wavered for a moment, and then he stood up straight.

"I trust you will allow me to take the noble path of a defeated enemy."

She never looked away from him, but when she spoke, it was so soft that only I could hear.

"Well, Rabbit?"

I jumped like my namesake, and it seemed as if time

stretched out like thread from a reel. It was her gift to me, the best she could do. She could not give me Sukai's life but, at the very least, she could give me the death of the Minister of the Left.

She was still even as the guards, the drovers, the attendants, and even the second-most important man in the empire waited. Not for her, though they did not know it, but for me.

It was a terrible gift, but in it I could see her heart, broken when she left the north and then reforged and made hard by the capital of Anh and the waters of Lake Scarlet. It was all she had, and she was giving it to me.

"Let him kill himself," I said finally. "As long as he is dead, that is all that matters to me."

That's something I think peasants understand better than nobles. For them, the way down matters, whether you are skewered by a dozen guardsmen or thrown in a silk sack to drown or allowed to remove your robe and walk down to the shores of the lake before you gut yourself. Peasants understand that dead is dead.

I did not want to watch him die. In-yo and Mai did, and they had the guards dispose of the mess while I stayed in Thriving Fortune. It already looked and felt different. Our days there were numbered.

There was a great deal to do after that, and I do not think that In-yo slept more than four hours each night.

She burned with a dry and fervent heat as the fortunes she cast over the last four years began to come true. There were reports to take and counter-insurrectionists to fight, and more than one assassination attempt to deal with.

One night, though, two nuns appeared from a southern order, and In-yo took me aside.

"He had no people that he ever told us about, and it is past time for him to be sent on his way. Will you come?"

Of course I would. There was already a small graveyard to the north of the house. An old maid was buried there, and she had recently been joined by two assassins. Now a burly silent man from the north dug a deep and narrow grave for Sukai, and as the nuns chanted sutras meant to guide him to what came next, we lowered his remnants into the ground.

I watched with dry eyes as they filled his grave, and then stones were placed over it to keep the beasts away. Mai carved a gravestone for him, marked with a sukai bird because she did not know how to write. It was fitting in a way, and you can go to see it yourself if you like.

I went into labor four weeks after we returned to Thriving Fortune. I began at dusk, and In-yo barred everyone from the chambers except herself and Mai. They hung a rope from the rafters that I pulled on when the pain was too great, and at dawn, with me delirious and half-insensible, a girl was born.

"Are you sure?" asked In-yo, and I nodded.

She and Mai cleaned me and the child, and while I slept, In-yo carried the baby out into the world, her daughter born of a miracle.

There is a story on the books, of the emperor of Anh coming to In-yo in a dream and pressing a seed into her belly. It is the story that the people of Anh like a great deal, about the great virility of their rulers and how they reach out in their sleep or in death, and it isn't as if the history books aren't full of such things.

With a little princess in her arms, and the mammoth guard of the north at her back, In-yo returned to the capital, and what happens next is a matter of record. She took the city with a minimum of bloodshed, and Emperor Sung killed himself or perhaps was killed by nobles who did not wish to see the dynasty humiliated. The crown prince was spirited away, the prince in exile until his own keepers killed him some years later. In-yo dealt as fairly as she could, was ruthless when she had to be, and the day after the eclipse of 359, which historians call the end of the Su Dynasty, she was crowned the Empress of Salt and Fortune, ruler of Anh and sister of the north.

The north took the south, and now, sixty years later, here we all are.

The story is over. Do you understand?

~

"I think I do now, Dowager Empress."

Slowly Chih knelt in front of Rabbit, pressing their forehead against the dusty wood.

"Oh, stop that now at once," Rabbit said. "If you know anything, you know why you must not do that."

Chih sat up again, nodding.

"I wanted to show you that I do understand. Honor is due to you as the mother of the Empress of Wheat and Flood, and honor is due to you as the friend of the Empress of Salt and Fortune."

"Look to your records, cleric. Honor is a light that brings trouble. Shadows are safer by far."

Chih dreamed that night of a young woman in servants' clothing walking through the dim halls of Thriving Fortune. As she went, she tidied the already tidy house, straightening a vase here, letting out a moth there. She looked around the compound with a sense of affection and nostalgia, but as she went outside and around to the north side of the house, her step quickened.

There was a young man waiting for her, leaning against a pile of rocks and tapping his foot in mock impatience. He was tall with gangling limbs and a face slightly out of true.

"Well, there you are, Rabbit. I thought rabbits were

meant to be fast, but look at how slow you are."

"Huh, like you're worth hurrying for? Don't flatter yourself. I was having a fine time in the capital."

In Chih's dream, the moon had set, leaving the star path traversed by the dead bright in the sky. The two of them looked up at it for a moment, and then they started to laugh, shaking their heads at the strangeness of the world, pain long behind them.

"Well, shall we?" asked the young man, and Rabbit shrugged.

"I hope the cleric locks up the house tightly after they go, but that's a small thing. Let's go."

They started to walk, rising as they did so, and from the porch over the lake, Chih watched them fade into two stars that shone just above the horizon.

Chapter Twelve

The next day, Chih woke to a triplet of rice balls on the sleeping mat next to them. They ate as they walked through the house, and as they'd guessed, Rabbit was nowhere to be found, not in the sleeping chambers or on the porch or in the small graveyard to the north.

Chih spent the morning circling the property, allowing Almost Brilliant to commit to memory what they could not to brush and paper, and finally, as their dream directed, they closed the doors and shutters of the house tightly before they walked back towards the road.

As they went, Almost Brilliant came to sit on their shoulder, pecking at their earlobe in a friendly way for a while before speaking.

"Well, that's done now. This could make your career for you."

"I suppose it could."

"You don't seem excited."

"I know what ambition feels like. This feels different. Like a weight around my shoulders, or a stone carried over my heart."

Almost Brilliant whistled, unconcerned.

"That must be duty, then. The Divine will be most pleased, Cleric Chih."

Chih shook their head. They walked east towards the capital, where in just nine days' time, the new empress would convene her first Dragon Court. She would defend her claim to the throne of Anh before all comers. Chih thought that even from the crowd, they would see in her face the trace of a migratory bird, a rabbit, and the empress from the north, fierce enough to fight wolves.

Acknowledgments

Thank you first to Ruoxi Chen, my superstar editor. She was the first person to ever lay eyes on this story, and she loved it so much she made me love it better.

Thank you to Diana Fox, my agent, for so many things!

Thank you to the team at Tor.com Publishing, without whom this manuscript would be a pile of printer paper I stapled together and left on the bus for people to find. Lauren Hougen, Mordicai Knode, Caroline Perny, Amanda Melfi, Christine Foltzer, and Irene Gallo, you are awesome!

Thank you to Alyssa Winans, artist extraordinaire, for understanding this story so well and putting that understanding into the cover. I don't think there's anything in all the world like seeing your very first book cover and knowing that the artist really got what you were trying to say.

Thank you to Ami Bedi, Cris Chingwa, Victoria Coy, Leah Kolman, Amy Lepke, and Meredy Shipp.

As for Shane Hochstetler, Carolyn Mulroney, and Grace Palmer: you guys know what you did. You've fed me, watched over me, worried about me, and generally made sure I didn't tip over into a ditch somewhere before my story got told. Thank you.

Writers spend a lot of time alone. If we're lucky, we like being alone, and if we're even luckier, we have people who love us through it all. As I write this, I can't even tell you how lucky I feel.

About the Author

Courtesy of the author

NGHI VO lives on the shores of Lake Michigan. Her short fiction has appeared in *Strange Horizons, Uncanny Magazine, PodCastle,* and *Lightspeed,* and her short story "Neither Witch nor Fairy" made the 2014 Tiptree Award Honor List. Nghi mostly writes about food, death, and family but sometimes detours into blood, love, and rhetoric. She believes in the ritual of lipstick, the power of stories, and the right to change your mind.

TOR·COM

**Science fiction. Fantasy. The universe.
And related subjects.**

*

More than just a publisher's website, *Tor.com*
is a venue for **original fiction, comics,** and
discussion of the entire field of SF and fantasy,
in all media and from all sources. Visit our site
today—and join the conversation yourself.